I WANT TO EAT YOUR BOOKS

I WANT TO EAT YOUR BOOKS

WRITTEN BY KARIN LEFRANC
ILLUSTRATED BY TYLER PARKER

Sky Pony Press
New York

Who's limping strangely down the hall
with outstretched arms and groaning drawl?
A ZOMBIE! Could it really be?
I hope he won't come after me!

"Oh no!" cries Eric. "Take a look.
He's chomping on your science book!"

"And now he's got
a paperback
he's munching as a
midday snack."

He looks at us with bulgy eyes
and chews a torn-off page and cries:

I WANT TO EAT YOUR BOOKS!

He rips a chunk off *Sharks at Sea*.
Non-fiction's now his cup of tea.

We look around for Mrs. Schmidt.
When she sees this, she'll have a fit.

This monster's not a carnivore.
The guy's a hungry book-ivore!
He wolfs my vocab book like cake.
(He'll learn the word for tummy ache!)

Cake (noun): A very big cupcake.

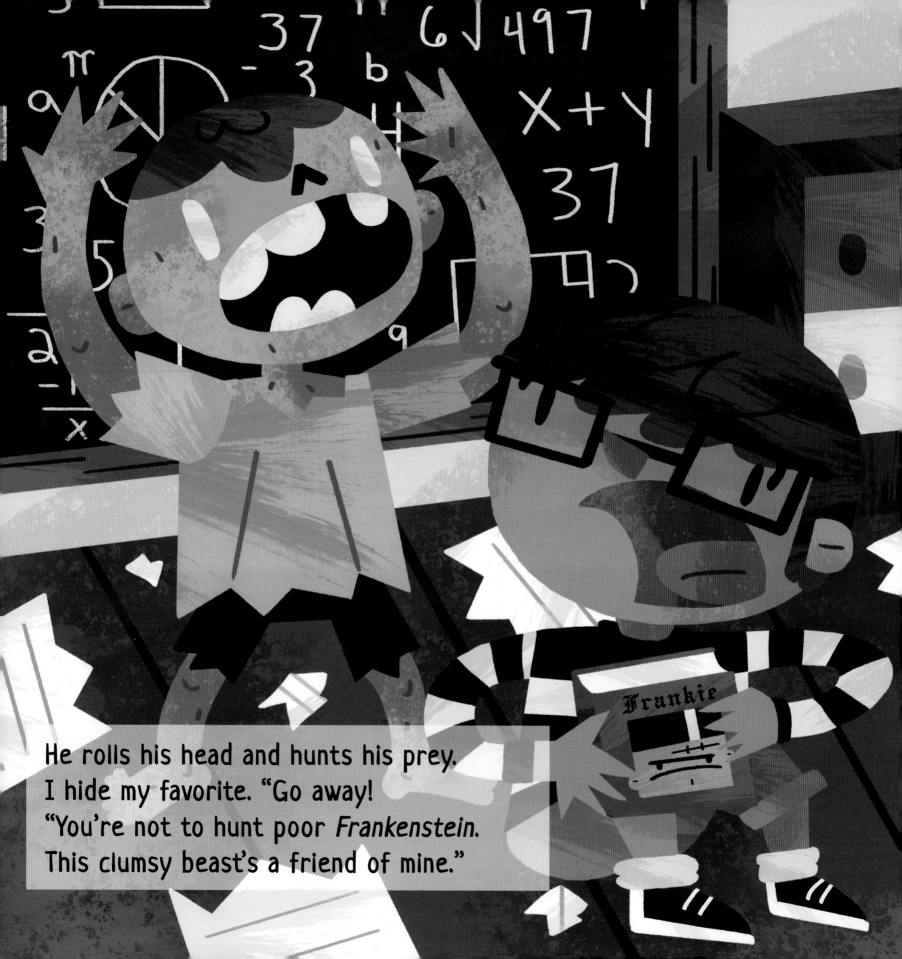

He rolls his head and hunts his prey.
I hide my favorite. "Go away!
"You're not to hunt poor *Frankenstein*.
This clumsy beast's a friend of mine."

Then just in time our teacher's here.
"It's Library!" And we all cheer.

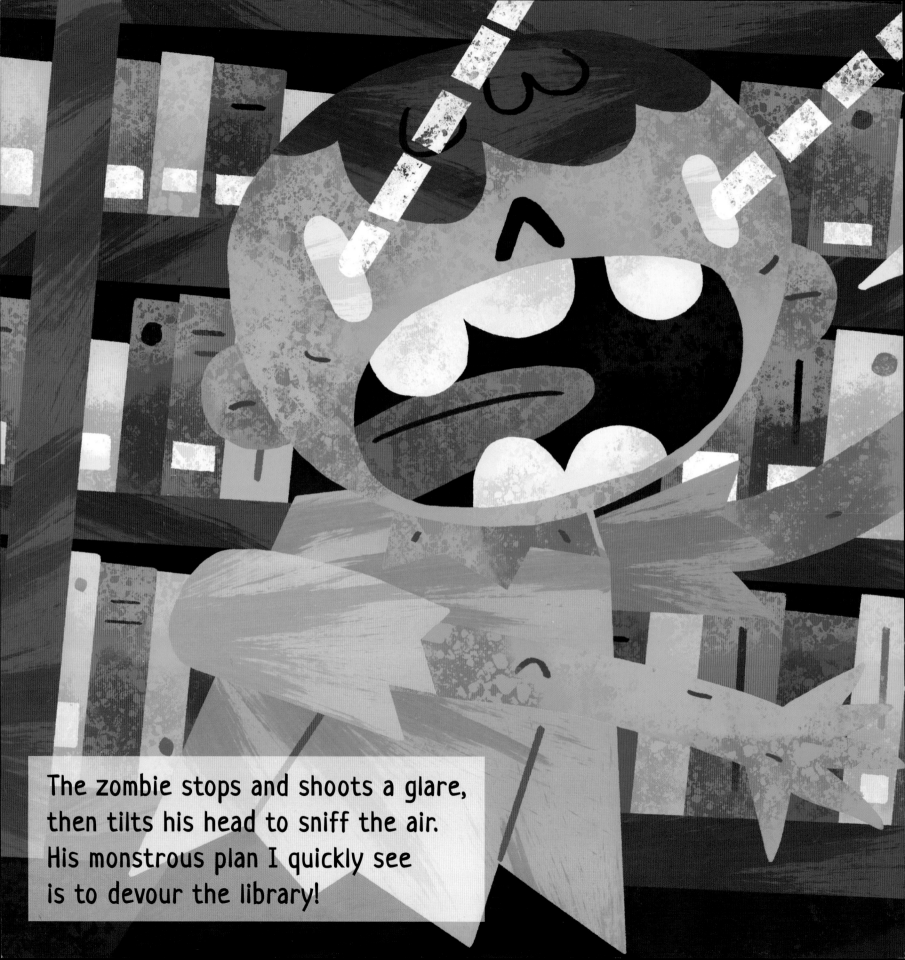

The zombie stops and shoots a glare,
then tilts his head to sniff the air.
His monstrous plan I quickly see
is to devour the library!

I WANT TO EAT YOUR BOOKS!

The creature marches down the aisle
and stops at Sci-Fi with a smile.
Such crispy pages strewn with words.
Our creature's craving seconds—thirds!

The Brain
Inside Out

This monster's diet is insane.
I spot the perfect book: *The Brain*.

I hold it up with shaking hand.
I hope our friend will understand.
He grunts and groans. Then grasps the book
and flips the page to take a look!

His fingers slide around the charts—
the human brain and all its parts.
The zombie drools with growing greed . . .
then taps the page and shouts,

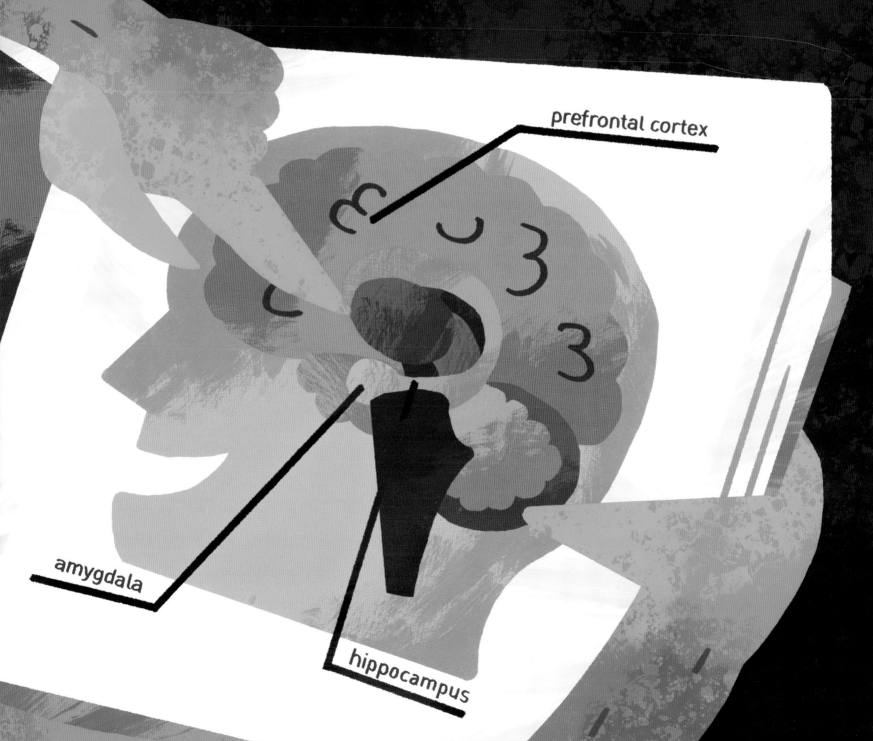

He listens, nods with little slurps,
and fills the air with paper

And then to everyone's surprise,
he shuffles up the row and cries:

I WANT TO READ YOUR BOOKS!

We hear a *riiip* and whirl around.
A real-life mummy's come unwound!

She's tearing sheets from *Easy Crafts*
to fill her holes and stop the drafts.
We need to stop this paper fight!
Then stunned, we see an awesome sight . . .

Our zombie's found a
box in white

and gently tapes the mummy tight.

We creep in closer for a look . . .

to find him reading her a book!

To my four little zombies—Madi, Beatrice, Josie, and Eric. —K. L.

Text Copyright © 2015 by Karin Lefranc
Illustration Copyright © 2015 by Tyler Parker

Sky Pony Press books may be purchased in bulk at special discounts for sales promotion, corporate gifts, fund-raising, or educational purposes. Special editions can also be created to specifications. For details, contact the Special Sales Department, Sky Pony Press, 307 West 36th Street, 11th Floor, New York, NY 10018 or info@ skyhorsepublishing.com.

Sky Pony® is a registered trademark of Skyhorse Publishing, Inc.®, a Delaware corporation.

Visit our website at www.skyponypress.com.

10 9 8 7 6 5 4 3 2 1

Manufactured in China, June 2015
This product conforms to CPSIA 2008

Library of Congress Cataloging-in-Publication Data

Lefranc, Karin.
   I want to eat your books / written by Karin Lefranc ; illustrated by Tyler Parker.
      pages cm
   Summary: "This zombie doesn't want to eat your brains--he wants to eat your books! Will the school library be devoured, or will the children discover something the zombie likes to do with books even more than eating them?"-- Provided by publisher.
   ISBN 978-1-63450-172-9 (hardback)
[1. Stories in rhyme. 2. Zombies--Fiction. 3. Books and reading--Fiction.] I. Parker, Tyler, illustrator. II. Title.
   PZ8.3.L526Iam 2015
   [E]--dc23
                        2015011258

Cover design by Sarah Brody
Cover illustration credit Tyler Parker

Thank you to my editor, Julie Matysik, and my agents, Liza Fleissig and Ginger Harris-Dontzin, for bringing this monster story to life!

Print ISBN: 978-1-63450-172-9
Ebook ISBN: 978-1-63450-920-6

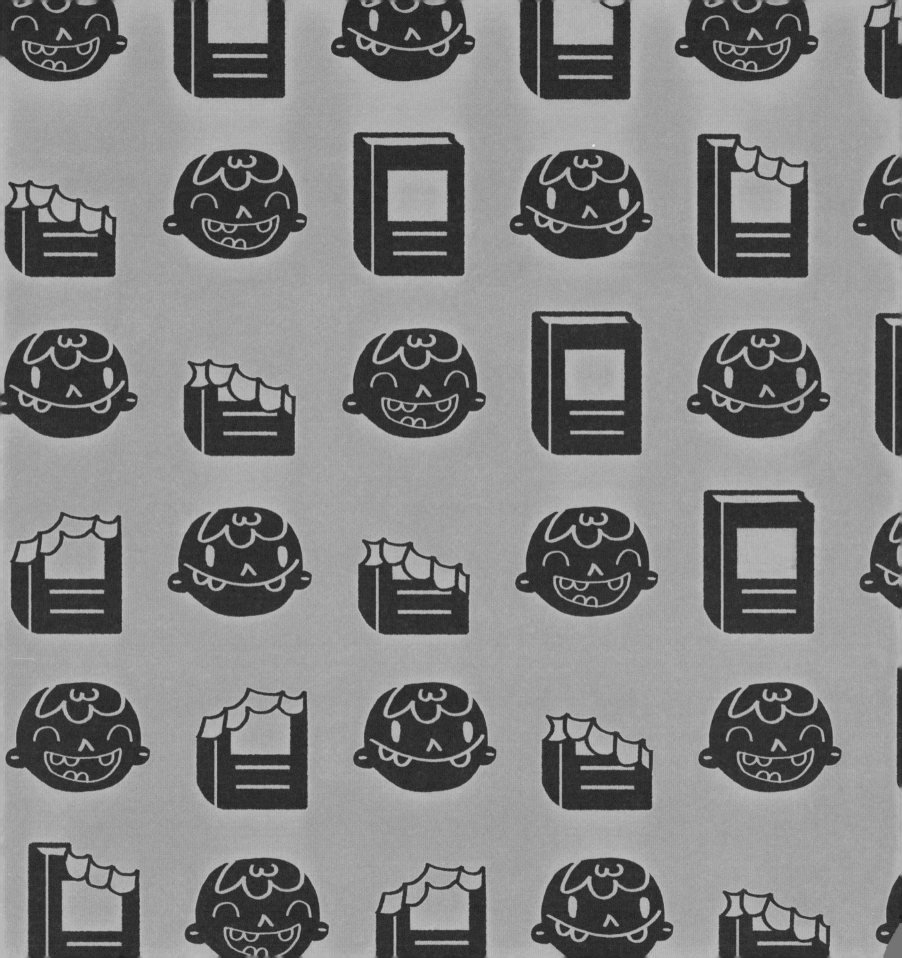